The Listerdale Mystery

by
Agatha Christie

Grand Magazine, Dec 1925

The Listerdale Mystery

I

Mrs St Vincent was adding up figures. Once or twice she sighed, and her hand stole to her aching forehead. She had always disliked arithmetic. It was unfortunate that nowadays her life should seem to be composed entirely of one particular kind of sum, the ceaseless adding together of small necessary items of expenditure making a total that never failed to surprise and alarm her.

Surely it couldn't come to that! She went back over the figures. She had made a trifling error in the pence, but otherwise the figures were correct.

Mrs St Vincent sighed again. Her headache by now was very bad indeed. She looked up as the door opened and her daughter Barbara came into the room. Barbara St Vincent was a very pretty girl; she had her mother's delicate features, and the same proud turn of the head, but her eyes were dark instead of blue, and she had a different mouth, a sulky red mouth not without attraction.

"Oh, Mother!" she cried. "Still juggling with those horrid old accounts? Throw them all into the fire."

"We must know where we are," said Mrs St Vincent uncertainly.

The girl shrugged her shoulders. "We're always in the same boat," she said dryly. "Damned hard up. Down to the last penny as usual."

Mrs St Vincent sighed.

"I wish-" she began, and then stopped.

"I must find something to do," said Barbara in hard tones. "And find it quickly. After all, I have taken that shorthand and typing course. So have about one million other girls from all I can see! 'What experience?' 'None, but-"Oh! Thank you, good morning. We'll let you know." But they never do! I must find some other kind of a job-any job."

"Not yet, dear," pleaded her mother. "Wait a little longer."

Barbara went to the window and stood looking out with unseeing eyes that took no note of the dingy line of houses opposite.

"Sometimes," she said slowly, "I'm sorry Cousin Amy took me with her to Egypt last winter. Oh! I know I had fun-about the only fun I've ever had or am likely to have in my life. I did enjoy myself-enjoyed myself thoroughly. But it was very unsettling. I mean-coming back to this."

She swept a hand round the room. Mrs St Vincent followed it with her eyes and winced. The room was typical of cheap furnished lodgings. A dusty aspidistra, showily ornamental furniture, a gaudy wallpaper faded in patches. There were signs that the personality of the tenants had struggled with that of the landlady; one or two pieces of good china, much cracked and mended, so that their saleable value was nil, a piece of embroidery thrown over the back of the sofa, a water colour sketch of a young girl in the fashion of twenty years ago, near enough still to Mrs St Vincent not to be mistaken.

"It wouldn't matter," continued Barbara, "if we'd never known anything else. But to think of Ansteys-"

She broke off, not trusting herself to speak of that dearly loved home which had belonged to the St Vincent family for centuries and which was now in the hands of strangers.

"If only Father-hadn't speculated-and borrowed-"

"My dear," said Mrs St Vincent. "Your father was never, in any sense of the word, a businessman."

She said it with a graceful kind of finality, and Barbara came over and gave her an aimless sort of kiss as she murmured, "Poor old Mums. I won't say anything."

Mrs St Vincent took up her pen again and bent over her desk. Barbara went back to the window. Presently the girl said: "Mother. I heard from-from Jim Masterton this morning. He wants to come and see me."

Mrs St Vincent laid down her pen and looked up sharply.

"Here?" she exclaimed.

"Well, we can't ask him to dinner at the Ritz very well," sneered Barbara.

Her mother looked unhappy. Again she looked round the room with innate distaste.

"You're right," said Barbara. "It's a disgusting place. Genteel poverty! Sounds all right-a whitewashed cottage in the country, shabby chintzes of good design, bowls of roses, crown Derby tea service that you wash up yourself. That's what it's like in books. In real life, with a son starting on the bottom rung of office life, it means London. Frowsy landladies, dirty children on the stairs, haddocks for breakfasts that aren't quite-quite and so on."

"If only-" began Mrs St Vincent. "But, really, I'm beginning to be afraid we can't afford even this room much longer."

"That means a bed-sitting-room-horror!-for you and me," said Barbara. "And a cupboard under the tiles for Rupert. And when Jim comes to call, I'll receive him in that dreadful room downstairs with tabbies all round the walls knitting, and stating at us, and coughing that dreadful kind of gulping cough they have!"

There was a pause.

"Barbara," said Mrs St Vincent at last. "Do you-I mean-would you-?"

She stopped, flushing a little. "You needn't be delicate, Mother," said Barbara. "Nobody is nowadays. Marry him, I suppose you mean? I would like a shot if he asked me. But I'm so awfully afraid he won't."

"Oh! Barbara, dear."

"Well, it's one thing seeing me out there with Cousin Amy, moving (as they say in novelettes) in the best society. He did take a fancy to me. Now he'll come here and see me in this! And he's a funny creature, you know, fastidious and old-fashioned. I-I rather like him for that. It reminds me of Ansteys and the village-everything a hundred years behind the times, but so-so-oh! I don't know-so fragrant. Like lavender!"

She laughed, half-ashamed of her eagerness. Mrs Vincent spoke with a kind of earnest simplicity.

"I should like you to marry Jim Masterton," she said. "He is-one of us. He is very well off, also, but that I don't mind about so much."

"I do," said Barbara. "I'm sick of being hard up."

"But, Barbara, it isn't-"

"Only for that? No. I do really. I-oh! Mother, can't you see I do?"

Mrs St Vincent looked very unhappy.

"I wish he could see you in your proper setting, darling," she said wistfully.

"Oh, well!" said Barbara. "Why worry? We might as well try and be cheerful about things. Sorry I've had such a grouch. Cheer up, darling."

She bent over her mother, kissed her forehead lightly, and went out. Mrs St Vincent, relinquishing all attempts at finance, sat down on the uncomfortable sofa. Her thoughts ran round in circles like squirrels in a cage.

"One may say what one likes, appearances do put a man off. Not later-not if they were really engaged. He'd know then what a sweet, dear girl she is. But it's so easy for young people to take the tone of their surroundings. Rupert, now, he's quite different from what he used to be. Not that I want my children to be stuck-up. That's not it a bit. But I should hate it if Rupert got engaged to that dreadful girl in the tobacconist's. I daresay she may be a very nice girl, really. But she's not our kind. It's all so difficult. Poor little Babs. If I could do anything-anything. But where's the money to come from? We've sold everything to give Rupert his start. We really can't even afford this."

To distract herself Mrs St Vincent picked up the Morning Post and glanced down the advertisements on the front page. Most of them she knew by heart. People who wanted capital, people who had capital and were anxious to dispose of it on note of hand alone, people who wanted to buy teeth (she always wondered why), people who wanted to sell furs and gowns and who had optimistic ideas on the subject of price.

Suddenly she stiffened to attention. Again and again she read the printed words.

"To gentlepeople only. Small house in Westminster, exquisitely furnished, offered to those who would really care for it. Rent purely nominal. No agents." A very ordinary advertisement. She had read many the same or-well, nearly the same. Nominal rent, that was where the trap lay.

Yet, since she was restless and anxious to escape from her thoughts, she put on her hat straightaway and took a convenient bus to the address given in the advertisement.

It proved to be that of a firm of house agents. Not a new bustling firm-a rather decrepit, old-fashioned place. Rather timidly she produced the advertisement, which she had torn out, and asked for particulars.

The white-haired old gentleman who was attending to her stroked his chin thoughtfully.

"Perfectly. Yes, perfectly, madam. That house, the house mentioned in the advertisement, is No. 7 Cheviot Place. You would like an order?"

"I should like to know the rent first?" said Mrs St Vincent. "Ah! The rent. The exact figure is not settled, but I can assure you that it is purely nominal."

"Ideas of what is purely nominal can vary," said Mrs St Vincent.

The old gentleman permitted himself to chuckle a little.

"Yes, that's an old trick-an old trick. But you can take my word for it, it isn't so in this case. Two or three guineas a week, perhaps, not more."

Mrs St Vincent decided to have the order. Not, of course, that there was any real likelihood of her being able to afford the place. But, after all, she might just see it. There must be some grave disadvantage attaching to it, to be offered at such a price. But her heart gave a little throb as she looked up at the outside of 7 Cheviot Place. A gem of a house. Queen Anne, and in perfect condition! A butler answered the door. He had grey hair and little side whiskers, and the meditative calm of an archbishop. A kindly archbishop, Mrs St Vincent thought.

He accepted the order with a benevolent air.

"Certainly, madam, I will show you over. The house is ready for occupation."

He went before her, opening doors, announcing rooms.

"The drawing room, the white study, a powder closet through here, madam."

It was perfect-a dream. The furniture all of the period, each piece with signs of wear, but polished with loving care. The loose rugs were of beautiful dim old colours. In each room were bowls of fresh flowers. The back of the house looked over the Green Park. The whole place radiated an old-world charm.

The tears came into Mrs St Vincent's eyes, and she fought them back with difficulty. So had Ansteys looked-Ansteys...

She wondered whether the butler had noticed her emotion. If so, he was too much the perfectly trained servant to show it. She liked these old servants, one felt safe with them, at ease. They were like friends.

"It is a beautiful house," she said softly. "Very beautiful. I am glad to have seen it."

"Is it for yourself alone, madam?"

"For myself and my son and daughter. But I'm afraid-"

She broke off. She wanted it so dreadfully-so dreadfully.

She felt instinctively that the butler understood. He did not look at her, as he said in a detached, impersonal way:

"I happen to be aware, madam, that the owner requires above all suitable tenants. The rent is of no importance to him. He wants the house to be tenanted by someone who will really care for and appreciate it."

"I should appreciate it," said Mrs St Vincent in a low voice.

She turned to go.

"Thank you for showing me over," she said courteously.

"Not at all, madam."

He stood in the doorway, very correct and upright as she walked away down the street. She thought to herself: "He knows. He's sorry for me. He's one of the old lot too. He'd like me to have it-not a labour member, or a button manufacturer! We're dying out, our sort, but we hang together."

In the end she decided not to go back to the agents. What was the good? She could afford the rent-but there were servants to be considered. There would have to be servants in a house like that.

The next morning a letter lay by her plate. It was from the house agents. It offered her the tenancy of 7 Cheviot Place for six months at two guineas a week, and went on: "You

11

have, I presume, taken into consideration the fact that the servants are remaining at the landlord's expense? It is really a unique offer."

It was. So startled was she by it, that she read the letter out. A fire of questions followed and she described her visit of yesterday.

"Secretive little Mums!" cried Barbara. "Is it really so lovely?"

Rupert cleared his throat and began a judicial cross-questioning.

"There's something behind all this. It's fishy, if you ask me. Decidedly fishy."

"So's my egg," said Barbara, wrinkling her nose. "Ugh! Why should there be something behind it? That's just like you, Rupert, always making mysteries out of nothing. It's those dreadful detective stories you're always reading."

"The rent's a joke," said Rupert. "In the city," he added importantly, "one gets wise to all sorts of queer things. I tell you, there's something very fishy about this business."

"Nonsense," said Barbara. "House belongs to a man with lots of money, he's fond of it, and he wants it lived in by decent people while he's away. Something of that kind. Money's probably no object to him."

"What did you say the address was?" asked Rupert of his mother.

"Seven Cheviot Place."

"Whew!" He pushed back his chair. "I say, this is exciting. That's the house Lord Listerdale disappeared from."

"Are you sure?" asked Mrs St Vincent doubtfully.

"Positive. He's got a lot of other houses all over London, but this is the one he lived in. He walked out of it one evening saying he was going to his club, and nobody ever saw him again. Supposed to have done a bunk to East Africa or somewhere like that, but nobody knows why. Depend upon it, he was murdered in that house. You say there's a lot of panelling?"

"Ye-es," said Mrs St Vincent faintly; "but-"

Rupert gave her no time. He went on with immense enthusiasm.

"Panelling! There you are. Sure to be a secret recess somewhere. Body's been stuffed in there and has been there ever since. Perhaps it was embalmed first."

"Rupert, dear, don't talk nonsense," said his mother.

"Don't be a double-dyed idiot," said Barbara. "You've been taking that peroxide blonde to the pictures too much."

Rupert rose with dignity-such dignity as his lanky and awkward age allowed, and delivered a final ultimatum.

"You take that house, Mums. I'll ferret out the mystery. You see if I don't."

Rupert departed hurriedly, in fear of being late at the office. The eyes of the two women met.

"Could we, Mother?" murmured Barbara tremulously. "Oh! If we could."

"The servants," said Mrs St Vincent pathetically, "would eat, you know. I mean, of course, one would want them to-but that's the drawback. One can so easily-just do without things-when it's only oneself."

She looked piteously at Barbara, and the girl nodded.

"We must think it over," said the mother.

But in reality her mind was made up. She had seen the sparkle in the girl's eyes. She thought to herself: "Jim Masterton must see her in proper surroundings. This is a chance-a wonderful chance. I must take it."

She sat down and wrote to the agents accepting their offer.

II

"Quentin, where did the lilies come from? I really can't buy expensive flowers."

"They were sent up from King's Cheviot, madam. It has always been the custom here."

The butler withdrew. Mrs St Vincent heaved a sigh of relief. What would she do without Quentin? He made everything so easy. She thought to herself: "It's too good to last. I shall wake up soon, I know I shall, and find it's been all a dream. I'm so happy here-two months already, and it's passed like a flash."

Life indeed had been astonishingly pleasant. Quentin, the butler, had displayed himself the autocrat of 7 Cheviot Place. "If you will leave everything to me, madam," he had said respectfully. "You will find it the best way."

Each week, he brought her the housekeeping books, their totals astonishingly low. There were only two other servants, a cook and a housemaid. They were pleasant in manner, and efficient in their duties, but it was Quentin who ran the house. Game and poultry appeared on the table sometimes, causing Mrs St Vincent solicitude. Quentin reassured her. Sent up from Lord Listerdale's country seat, King's Cheviot, or from his Yorkshire moor. "It has always been the custom, madam."

Privately Mrs St Vincent doubted whether the absent Lord Listerdale would agree with those words. She was inclined to suspect Quentin of usurping his master's authority. It was clear that he had taken a fancy to them, and that in his eyes nothing was too good for them.

Her curiosity aroused by Rupert's declaration, Mrs St Vincent had made a tentative reference to Lord Listerdale when she next interviewed the house agents. The white-haired old gentleman had responded immediately.

"Yes, Lord Listerdale was in East Africa, had been there for the last eighteen months."

"Our client is rather an eccentric man," he had said, smiling broadly. "He left London in a most unconventional manner, as you may perhaps remember? Not a word to anyone. The newspapers got hold of it. There were actually inquiries on foot at Scotland Yard. Luckily, news was received from Lord Listerdale himself from East Africa. He invested his cousin, Colonel Carfax, with power of attorney. It is the latter who conducts all Lord Listerdale's affairs. Yes, rather eccentric, I fear. He has always been a great traveller in the wilds-it is quite on the cards that he may not return for years to England, though he is getting on in years."

"Surely he is not so very old," said Mrs St Vincent, with a sudden memory of a bluff, bearded face, rather like an Elizabethan sailor, which she had once noticed in an illustrated magazine.

"Middle-aged," said the white-haired gentleman. "Fifty-three, according to Debrett."

This conversation Mrs St Vincent had retailed to Rupert with the intention of rebuking that young gentleman.

Rupert, however, was undismayed.

"It looks fishier than ever to me," he had declared. "Who's this Colonel Carfax? Probably comes into the title if anything happens to Listerdale. The letter from East Africa was probably forged. In three years, or whatever it is, this Carfax will presume death, and take the title. Meantime, he's got all the handling of the estate. Very fishy, I call it."

He had condescended graciously to approve the house. In his leisure moments he was inclined to tap the panelling and make elaborate measurements for the possible location of a secret room, but little by little his interest in the mystery of Lord Listerdale abated. He was also less enthusiastic on the subject of the tobacconist's daughter. Atmosphere tells.

To Barbara the house had brought great satisfaction. Jim Masterton had come home, and was a frequent visitor. He and Mrs St Vincent got on splendidly together, and he said something to Barbara one day that startled her. "This house is a wonderful setting for your mother, you know."

"For Mother?"

"Yes. It was made for her! She belongs to it in an extraordinary way. You know there's something queer about this house altogether, something uncanny and haunting."

"Don't get like Rupert," Barbara implored him. "He is convinced that the wicked Colonel Carfax murdered Lord Listerdale and hid his body under the floor."

Masterton laughed.

"I admire Rupert's detective zeal. No, I didn't mean anything of that kind. But there's something in the air, some atmosphere that one doesn't quite understand."

They had been three months in Cheviot Place when Barbara came to her mother with a radiant face. "Jim and I-we're engaged. Yes-last night. Oh, Mother! It all seems like a fairy tale come true."

"Oh, my dear! I'm so glad-so glad."

Mother and daughter clasped each other close.

"You know Jim's almost as much in love with you as he is with me," said Barbara at last, with a mischievous laugh.

Mrs St Vincent blushed very prettily.

"He is," persisted the girl. "You thought this house would make such a beautiful setting for me, and all the time it's really a setting for you. Rupert and I don't quite belong here. You do."

"Don't talk nonsense, darling."

"It's not nonsense. There's a flavour of enchanted castle about it, with you as an enchanted princess and Quentin as-as-oh!- a benevolent magician."

Mrs St Vincent laughed and admitted the last item.

Rupert received the news of his sister's engagement very calmly.

"I thought there was something of the kind in the wind," he observed sapiently.

He and his mother were dining alone together. Barbara was out with Jim.

Quentin placed the port in front of him and withdrew noiselessly.

"That's a rum old bird," said Rupert, nodding towards the closed door. "There's something odd about him, you know, something-"

"Not fishy?" interrupted Mrs St Vincent, with a faint smile.

"Why, Mother, how did you know what I was going to say?" demanded Rupert in all seriousness.

"It's rather a word of yours, darling. You think everything is fishy. I suppose you have an idea that it was Quentin who did away with Lord Listerdale and put him under the floor?"

"Behind the panelling," corrected Rupert. "You always get things a little bit wrong, Mother. No, I've inquired about that. Quentin was down at King's Cheviot at the time."

Mrs St Vincent smiled at him, as she rose from the table and went up to the drawing room. In some ways Rupert was a long time growing up.

Yet a sudden wonder swept over her for the first time as to Lord Listerdale's reasons for leaving England so abruptly. There must be something behind it, to account for that sudden decision. She was still thinking the matter over when Quentin came in with the coffee tray, and she spoke out impulsively. "You have been with Lord Listerdale a long time, haven't you, Quentin?"

"Yes, madam; since I was a lad of twenty-one. That was in the late Lord's time. I started as third footman."

"You must know Lord Listerdale very well. What kind of a man is he?"

The butler turned the tray a little, so that she could help herself to sugar more conveniently, as he replied in even unemotional tones:

"Lord Listerdale was a very selfish gentleman, madam; with no consideration for others."

He removed the tray and bore it from the room. Mrs St Vincent sat with her coffee cup in her hand and a puzzled frown on her face. Something struck her as odd in the speech apart from the views it expressed. In another minute it flashed home to her.

Quentin had used the word "was," not "is." But then, he must think-must believe-She pulled herself up. She was as bad as Rupert! But a very definite uneasiness assailed her. Afterwards she dated her first suspicions from that moment.

With Barbara's happiness and future assured, she had time to think her own thoughts, and against her will, they began to centre round the mystery of Lord Listerdale. What was the real story? Whatever it was, Quentin knew something about it. Those had been odd words of his-"a very selfish gentleman-no consideration for others." What lay behind them? He had spoken as a judge might speak, detachedly and impartially.

Was Quentin involved in Lord Listerdale's disappearance? Had he taken an active part in any tragedy there might have been? After all, ridiculous as Rupert's assumption had seemed at the time, that single letter with its power of attorney coming from East Africa was-well, open to suspicion.

But try as she would, she could not believe any real evil of Quentin. Quentin, she told herself over and over again, was good - she used the word as simply as a child might have done. Quentin was good. But he knew something!

She never spoke with him again of his master. The subject was apparently forgotten. Rupert and Barbara had other things to think of, and there were no further discussions.

It was towards the end of August that her vague surmises crystallized into realities. Rupert had gone for a fortnight's holiday with a friend who had a motorcycle and trailer. It was some ten days after his departure that Mrs St Vincent was startled to see him rush into the room where she sat writing.

"Rupert!" she exclaimed.

"I know, Mother. You didn't expect to see me for another three days. But something's happened. Anderson- my pal, you know-didn't much care where he went, so I suggested having a look in at King's Cheviot-"

"King's Cheviot? But why -?"

"You know perfectly well, Mother, that I've always scented something fishy about things here. Well, I had a look at the old place-it's let, you know-nothing there. Not that I actually expected to find anything-I was just nosing round, so to speak."

Yes, she thought, Rupert was very like a dog at this moment. Hunting in circles for something vague and undefined, led by instinct, busy and happy.

"It was when we were passing through a village about eight or nine miles away that it happened-that I saw him, I mean."

"Saw whom?"

"Quentin-just going into a little cottage. Something fishy here, I said to myself, and we stopped the bus, and I went back. I rapped on the door and he himself opened it."

"But I don't understand. Quentin hasn't been away-"

"I'm coming to that, Mother. If you'd only listen and not interrupt. It was Quentin, and it wasn't Quentin, if you know what I mean."

Mrs St Vincent clearly did not know, so he elucidated matters further.

"It was Quentin all right, but it wasn't our Quentin. It was the real man."

"Rupert!"

"You listen. It was taken in myself at first, and said: 'It is Quentin, isn't it?' And the old Johnny said: 'Quite right, sir, that is my name. What can I do for you?' And then I saw that it wasn't our man, though it was precious like him, voice and all. I asked a few questions, and it all came out. The old chap hadn't an idea of anything fishy being on. He'd been butler to Lord Listerdale, all right, and was retired on a pension and given this cottage just about the time that Lord Listerdale was supposed to have gone off to Africa. You see where that leads us. This man's an impostor-he's playing the part of Quentin for purposes of his own. My theory is that he came up to town that evening, pretending to be the butler from King's Cheviot, got an interview with Lord Listerdale, killed him and hid his body behind the panelling. It's an old house, there's sure to be a secret recess-"

"Oh, don't let's go into all that again," interrupted Mrs St Vincent wildly. "I can't bear it. Why should he-that's what I want to know-why? If he did such a thing-which I don't believe for one minute, mind you-what was the reason for it all?"

"You're right," said Rupert. "Motive-that's important. Now I've made inquiries. Lord Listerdale had a lot of house property. In the last two days I've discovered that practically every one of these houses of his have been let in the last eighteen months to people like ourselves for a merely nominal rent-and with the proviso that the servants should remain. And in every case Quentin himself-the man calling himself Quentin, I mean-has been there for part of the time as butler. That looks as though there were something-jewels, or papers-secreted in one of Lord Listerdale's houses, and the gang doesn't know which. I'm assuming a gang, but of course this fellow Quentin may be in it single-handed. There's a-"

Mrs St Vincent interrupted him with a certain amount of determination:

"Rupert! Do stop talking for one minute. You're making my head spin. Anyway, what you are saying is nonsense-about gangs and hidden papers."

"There's another theory," admitted Rupert. "This Quentin may be someone that Lord Listerdale has injured. The real butler told me a long story about a man called Samuel Lowe-an undergardener he was, and about the same height and build as Quentin himself. He'd got a grudge against Listerdale-"

Mrs St Vincent started.

"With no consideration for others." The words came back to her mind in their passionless, measured accents. Inadequate words, but what might they not stand for?

In her absorption she hardly listened to Rupert. He made a rapid explanation of something that she did not take in, and went hurriedly from the room. Then she woke up. Where had Rupert gone? What was he going to do? She had not caught his last words. Perhaps he was going for the police. In that case-

She rose abruptly and rang the bell. With his usual promptness, Quentin answered it.

"You rang, madam?"

"Yes. Come in, please, and shut the door."

The butler obeyed, and Mrs St Vincent was silent a moment while she studied him with earnest eyes.

She thought: "He's been kind to me-nobody knows how kind. The children wouldn't understand. This wild story of Rupert's may be all nonsense-On the other hand, there may-yes, there may-be something in it. Why should one judge? One can't know. The rights and wrongs of it, I mean... And I'd stake my life-yes, I would!- on his being a good man."

Flushed and tremulous, she spoke.

"Quentin, Mr Rupert has just got back. He has been down to King's Cheviot-to a village near there-"

She stopped, noticing the quick start he was not able to conceal.

"He has-seen someone," she went on in measured accents.

She thought to herself: "There-he's warned. At any rate, he's warned."

After that first quick start, Quentin had resumed his unruffled demeanour, but his eyes were fixed on her face, watchful and keen, with something in them she had not seen there before. They were, for the first time, the eyes of a man and not of a servant.

He hesitated for a minute, then said in a voice which also had subtly changed:

"Why do you tell me this, Mrs St Vincent?"

Before she could answer, the door flew open and Rupert strode into the room. With him was a dignified middle-aged man with little side whiskers and the air of a benevolent archbishop. Quentin!

"Here he is," said Rupert. "The real Quentin. I had him outside in the taxi. Now, Quentin, look at this man and tell me-is he Samuel Lowe?"

It was for Rupert a triumphant moment. But it was short-lived; almost at once he scented something wrong. For while the real Quentin was looking abashed and highly uncomfortable, the second Quentin was smiling a broad smile of undisguised enjoyment.

He slapped his embarrassed duplicate on the back.

"It's all right, Quentin. Got to let the cat out of the bag sometime, I suppose. You can tell 'em who I am."

The dignified stranger drew himself up.

"This, sir," he announced in a reproachful tone, "is my master, Lord Listerdale, sir."

The next minute beheld many things. First, the complete collapse of the cocksure Rupert. Before he knew what was happening, his mouth still open from the shock of the discovery, he found himself being gently manoeuvred towards the door, a friendly voice that was, and yet was not, familiar in his ear.

"It's quite all right, my boy. No bones broken. But I want a word with your mother. Very good work of yours, to ferret me out like this."

He was outside on the landing gazing at the shut door. The real Quentin was standing by his side, a gentle stream of explanation flowing from his lips. Inside the room Lord Listerdale was fronting Mrs St Vincent.

"Let me explain-if I can! I've been a selfish devil all my life-the fact came home to me one day. I thought I'd try a little altruism for a change, and being a fantastic kind of fool, I started my career fantastically. I'd sent subscriptions to odd things, but I felt the need of doing something-well, something personal. I've been sorry always for the class that can't beg, that must suffer in silence-poor gentlefolk. I have a lot of house property. I conceived the idea of leasing these houses to people who-well, needed and appreciated them. Young couples with their way to make, widows with sons and daughters starting in the world. Quentin has been more than butler to me; he's a friend. With his consent and assistance I borrowed his personality. I've always had a talent for acting. The idea came to me on my way to the club one night, and I went straight off to talk it over with Quentin. When I found they were making a fuss about my disappearance, I arranged that a letter should come from me in East Africa. In it, I gave full instructions to my cousin, Maurice Carfax. And-well, that's the long and short of it."

He broke off rather lamely, with an appealing glance at Mrs St Vincent. She stood very straight, and her eyes met his steadily.

"It was a kind plan," she said. "A very unusual one, and one that does you credit. I am-most grateful. But-of course, you understand that we cannot stay?"

"I expected that," he said. "Your pride won't let you accept what you'd probably style 'charity.'"

"Isn't that what it is?" she asked steadily.

"No," he answered. "Because I ask something in exchange."

"Something?"

"Everything." His voice rang out, the voice of one accustomed to dominate.

"When I was twenty-three," he went on, "I married the girl I loved. She died a year later. Since then I have been very lonely. I have wished very much I could find a certain lady-the lady of my dreams..."

"Am I that?" she asked, very low. "I am so old-so faded."

He laughed.

"Old? You are younger than either of your children. Now I am old, if you like."

But her laugh rang out in turn, a soft ripple of amusement. "You? You are a boy still. A boy who loves to dress up!" She held out her hands and he caught them in his.